THE BIG BEACH CLEANUP

CHARLOTTE OFFSAY ILLUSTRATED BY **KATIE REWSE**

Albert Whitman & Company
Chicago, Illinois

CORA HAD BIG PLANS.

She was going to be the Crystal Beach Sandcastle Champion.

She would spend all summer practicing—

tall ones,

funny ones,

and ones that made you
want to pack up your
bags and move on in.

But when she reached the beach,
her plans went out with the tide.

"Oh no!"

Cora ran onto the sand and started digging anyway.

Trash tumbled into her bucket.

Cora frowned. "Can you fix it, Mama?"

"I wish I could. I don't have enough hands."

Cora slipped her hand into Mama's.
"One, two, three, four. Is four enough?"

Mama grabbed gloves from her truck and handed a pair to Cora.

Together they walked up and down the beach.

"How did this happen?" asked Cora.

"It probably washed up from the ocean," said Mama.

"The ocean makes trash?"

Mama shook her head. "When trash is dropped outside, it can fall into a drain that empties onto the beach or into the ocean. Then some trash washes onto shore."

Dark clouds gathered overhead. "It's time to head home," said Mama.

Cora's feet dragged. Would they ever clear enough room to save the contest? Four hands weren't enough.

"I'm sorry," said Mama. "There'll be other contests."

"Not if nobody cleans the beach," grumbled Cora.

Cora's grumbling didn't last long.
When they arrived home and saw Grandpa,
Cora cried, "Look, more hands!"

The next day, Cora counted six helping
hands on the way to the beach.

But when they arrived,

it looked as though Cora hadn't cleaned a thing.

Mama hummed as she worked, but Cora's bucket felt heavy.

"How about a sandcastle break?" suggested Grandpa.

Cora plopped down.

"Oh no!" cried Cora. "That bird is eating trash!"

"It doesn't know any better," said Grandpa.
"Sometimes animals confuse trash for food."

The bird hopped toward another wrapper.

Cora sighed and kicked the sand.
"Six hands aren't enough."

Then, as the sand settled,
she spotted...

an idea.

At home, Cora and Mama got started right away.

They posted flyers at the market,
the library,
and the ice-cream shop.

Cora grinned at the line outside the ice-cream shop. With all these hands the beach would be clean in no time.

But as Cora stood outside, her grin faded.

Person after person walked right past her outstretched hand.

"Mama, why isn't anyone taking my flyers?"

Before Mama could answer,

Cora spotted her neighbor.

"Molly! Will you help us?"

"Sorry, I'm working this summer," said Molly.

Cora's eyes stung as Molly turned away.

"People are busy," said Mama, "but there are lots of ways for them to help, like not littering, or saying no to things we use only once, like straws, so that less trash ends up in the ocean."

Cora nodded and wiped her eyes. "Their hands are still helping."

So Cora kept on asking.

She talked to her friends, visited her neighbors, and spread the word.

"Mama! We've got eight hands!"

"Ten hands!"

"Twelve hands!"

And slowly...

more

and more

and more hands joined together.

News of the efforts at Crystal Beach spread, and eventually a new flyer appeared.

On the day of the sandcastle competition,
people built tall ones,
funny ones,
and ones that made you want to pack up
your bags and move on in.

And even though Cora's
sandcastle didn't win,
her heart swelled with pride.

It was just the beginning.

Cora had big plans.

AUTHOR'S NOTE

There is a lot of work to be done to prevent trash from ending up in the ocean. But big changes start with small steps. Like Cora, you can make a difference.

* Put trash in the trash can, and ask those around you to do the same.
* Ask your household to use reusable products whenever possible. For example, pack a refillable bottle instead of a disposable one, and use reusable bags for your snacks.
* Say no to single-use items and disposable plastics, like straws, Styrofoam containers, plastic bags, and plastic utensils.
* Many stores use paper bags instead of plastic, or even require customers to bring their own bags. If your local store doesn't, suggest that they start. Some towns and cities have even banned stores from providing plastic bags to customers. If yours hasn't, talk to your grown-up about starting a petition.
* Ask local restaurants to stop using straws or to swap them out for environmentally friendly ones.
* Pop balloons after you are done playing with them, and put them in the trash.
* Cut plastic six-pack rings before putting them in the trash.
* Animals create their own garbage. Be sure to clean up after your pet so that their waste ends up in a trash can instead of a storm drain.
* Help keep storm drains clean.
* Buy recycled products.
* Talk to your school and neighbors about how to recycle and dispose of trash properly.

DID YOU KNOW...?

* Around half of all plastic items are used only once.
* According to a 2015 study by researchers at Plymouth University in the UK, nearly seven hundred different kinds of marine animals have eaten or gotten stuck in plastic.
* When animals mistake trash for food, their stomachs can feel full, so they stop eating actual food that keeps them healthy.
* According to a study published in the journal *Science* in February 2015, every year enough trash ends up in the ocean to line the entire world's coastline with grocery bags full of trash—five times over.

I would like to thank Nancy Shrodes, Associate Director of Policy and Outreach with Heal the Bay, and Sarah Kollar, Project and Outreach Manager of the International Coastal Cleanup with Ocean Conservancy, for generously lending their expertise to this book.

I would also like to thank my editor, Christina Pulles, my supportive agent, Nicole Geiger, and my incredible writing community for believing in this book and bringing it to life. —CO

For Eliana
and Thomas, who
inspired this book
—CO

For Dean
—KR

Library of Congress Cataloging-in-Publication data is on file with the publisher.

Text copyright © 2021 by Charlotte Offsay
Illustrations copyright © 2021 by Albert Whitman & Company
Illustrations by Katie Rewse
First published in the United States of America in 2021 by Albert Whitman & Company
ISBN 978-0-8075-0801-5 (hardcover)
ISBN 978-0-8075-0810-7 (ebook)

Printed in China
10 9 8 7 6 5 4 3 2 1 WKT 24 23 22 21 20

Design by Aphelandra

For more information about Albert Whitman & Company,
visit our website at www.albertwhitman.com.